This book belongs to

_____

_____

Henry and Mudge
Best Friends

Story by Cynthia Rylant
Pictures by Suçie Stevenson

POCKET
B O O K S

First published in Great Britain by Simon & Schuster UK Ltd, 2001
This edition first published by Pocket Books, 2001
An imprint of Simon & Schuster UK Ltd
A Viacom Company

Text copyright © Cynthia Rylant, 1987
Illustrations copyright © Suçie Stevenson, 1987

Simon & Schuster UK Ltd
Africa House
64-78 Kingsway
London WC2B 6AH

Simon & Schuster Australia
Sydney

A CIP catalogue record for this book is available from the British Library

ISBN 07434 15930

1 3 5 7 9 10 8 6 4 2

Printed in Hong Kong

These stories were first published separately in the USA by Aladdin Papers in 1990.

Contents

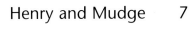

Henry

Henry had no brothers
and no sisters.
'I want a brother,'
he told his parents.
'Sorry,' they said.
Henry had no friends
on his street.

'I want to live
on a different street,"
he told his parents.
'Sorry,' they said.
Henry had no pets
at home.
'I want to have a dog,'
he told his parents
'Sorry,' they *almost* said.

But first they looked
at their house
with no brothers and sisters.
Then they looked
at their street
with no children.
Then they looked
at Henry's face.

Then they looked at each other.
'Okay,' they said.
'I want to hug you!'
Henry told his parents.
And he did.

Mudge

Henry searched for a dog
'Not just any dog,' said Henry.
'Not a short one,' he said.
'Not a curly one,' he said.
'And no pointed ears.'

Then he found Mudge.
Mudge had floppy ears,
not pointed.
And Mudge had straight fur,
not curly.
But Mudge was short.
'Because he's a puppy,'
Henry said.
'He'll grow.'

And did he ever!
He grew out of his puppy box.
He grew out of his dog box.

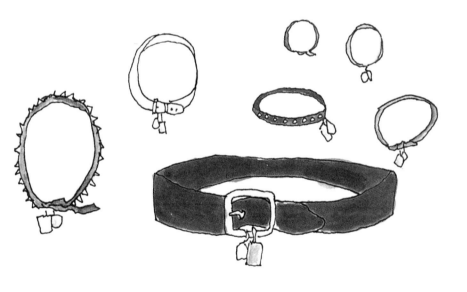

He grew out of seven collars
in a row.
And when he finally
stopped growing ...

he weighed eighty kilograms,
he stood one metre tall,
and he drooled.
'I'm glad you're not short,'
Henry said.

And Mudge licked him,
then sat on him.

Henry

Henry used to walk
to school alone.
When he walked
he used to worry about
tornadoes,
ghosts,
biting dogs,
and bullies.

He walked as fast
as he could.
He looked straight ahead.
He never looked back.
But now he walked to school
with Mudge.

And now when he walked,
he thought about
vanilla ice cream,
rain,
rocks,
and good dreams.
He walked to school
but not too fast.
He walked to school
and sometimes backwards.

He walked to school
and patted Mudge's big head,
happy.

Mudge

Mudge loved Henry's room.
He loved the dirty socks.
He loved the teddy bear.
He loved the fish tank.
But mostly he loved
Henry's bed.

Because in Henry's bed
was Henry.
Mudge loved to climb in
with Henry.
Then he loved
to smell him.

He smelled his lemon hair
He smelled his milky mouth.
He smelled his soapy ears.
He smelled his chocolate fingers.

Then he put his head
by Henry's head.
He looked at the fish tank.
He looked at the bear.
He looked at Henry.
He licked him.
And he fell asleep.

Mudge

One day Mudge took a walk
without Henry.
The sun was shining,
the birds were flying,
the grass smelled sweet.
Mudge couldn't wait for Henry.
So he left.

He went down one road,
sniffing the bushes,
then down another road,
kicking up dust.
He went through a field,
across a stream,
into some pine trees.

And when he came out
on the other side,
he was lost.

He couldn't smell Henry.
He couldn't smell
his front door.
He couldn't smell
the street he lived on.
Mudge looked all around
and didn't see anything
or anyone
he knew.

He whined a little,
alone without Henry.
Then he lay down,
alone without Henry.
He missed Henry's bed.

Henry thought Mudge
would be with him always.
He thought Mudge
made everything safe.
He thought Mudge
would never go away.

30

And when Mudge did go away,
when Henry called and called
but Mudge didn't come,
Henry's heart hurt
and he cried for an hour.
But when he finished crying,
Henry said, 'Mudge loves me.
He wouldn't leave.
He must be lost.'

So Henry walked and walked,
and he called and called,
and he looked and looked
for his dog Mudge.
He walked down one road,
then down another road.
The sun shone as Henry ran
through a field,
calling and calling.

The birds flew past
as he stood beside a stream,
calling and calling.

And the tears fell again
as he looked at the
empty pine trees
for his lost dog.
'*Mudge!*' he called, one last time.

And Mudge woke up
from his lonely sleep,
then
came
running.

Every day when Henry woke up,
he saw Mudge's big head.
And every day
when Mudge woke up,
he saw Henry's small face.

They ate breakfast
at the same time;

they ate dinner
at the same time.

And when Henry was at school,
Mudge just lay around
and waited.
Mudge never went for a walk
without Henry again.
And Henry never worried
that Mudge would leave.

Because sometimes, in their dreams,
they saw long silent roads,
big wide fields,
deep streams,
and pine trees.

In those dreams,
Mudge was alone
and Henry was alone.
So when Mudge woke up
and knew Henry was with him,
he remembered the dream
and stayed closer.

And when Henry woke up
and knew Mudge was with him,
he remembered the dream
and the looking
and the calling
and the fear
and he knew
he would never lose Mudge
again.

The Snow Glory

When the snow melted
and Spring came,
Henry and his big dog Mudge
stayed outside
all the time.

Henry had missed
riding his bike.
Mudge had missed
chewing on sticks.
They were glad
it was warmer.

One day when Henry and Mudge
were in their garden,
Henry saw something blue
on the ground.
He got closer to it.
'Mudge!' he called.
'It's a flower!'
Mudge slowly walked over
and sniffed the blue flower.

Then he sneezed all over Henry. 'Aw, Mudge,' Henry said.

Later, Henry's mother
told him that the flower
was called a snow glory.
'Can I pick it?'
Henry asked.
'Oh, no,' said his mother.
'Let it grow.'
So Henry didn't pick it.

Every day he saw the snow glory
in the garden,
blue
and looking so pretty.
He knew he shouldn't pick it.
He was trying not to pick it.
But he thought how nice
it would look in a jar.
He thought how nice
to bring it inside.
He thought how nice
it would be
to own that snow glory.
Every day he stood with Mudge
and looked at the flower.

Mudge would stick his nose
into the grass
all around the snow glory.
But he never looked at it
the way Henry did.
'Don't you think the snow glory
has been growing long enough?'
Henry would ask his mother.
'Let it grow, Henry,'
she would say.

Oh, Henry wanted that snow glory.
And one day
he just knew
he had to have it.
So he took Mudge
by the collar
and he stood
beside the snow glory.

'I'm going to pick it,'
Henry whispered to Mudge.
'I've let it grow a long time.'
Henry bent his head and
he said in Mudge's ear,
'Now I *need* it.'
And Mudge wagged his tail,
licked Henry's face,
then put his big mouth
right over that snow glory…

and he ate it.
'No, *Mudge*!' Henry said.
But too late.
There was a blue flower
in Mudge's belly.

'I said *need* it, not *eat* it!'
shouted Henry.
He was so cross because
Mudge took his flower.
It was Henry's flower
and Mudge took it.

And Henry almost said,
'Bad dog,' but he stopped.

He looked at Mudge,
who looked back at him
with soft brown eyes
and a flower in his belly.

Henry knew it wasn't his snow glory.
He knew it wasn't anybody's snow glory.
Just a thing to let grow.
And if someone ate it,
it was just a thing to let go.
Henry stopped feeling cross.

He put his arms around
Mudge's big head.

'Next time, Mudge,'
he said,
'try to *listen* better.'
Mudge wagged his tail
and licked his lips.
One blue petal
fell from his mouth
into Henry's hand.
Henry smiled,
put it in his pocket,
and they went inside.

Puddle Trouble

In April
it rained
day after day
after day
after day.

Henry was getting bored.
Mudge was chewing up
everything in the house.
So Henry said,
'Let's play outside anyway.'

He put on his raincoat
and shoes
and went outside with Mudge.
Henry forgot to ask his father
if it was all right.

When Mudge stepped
into the wet grass,
he lifted his paws
and shook them.
'Too bad you don't
have shoes,' Henry said.
And he walked in a circle
around Mudge.
Squish, squish, squish, squish.

Mudge listened
and looked at Henry.
Then he got closer
to Henry
and wagged his tail
and shook the water from
his big wet furry body
all over Henry.
Henry wiped the water
from his face.
'Aw, Mudge,' he said.

The two of them
went walking.
And down the road
they found a big puddle.
A giant puddle.
A lake puddle.
An ocean puddle.
And Henry said, 'Wow!'

He started running.
Mudge got there first.
SPLASH!
Muddy water all over Mudge.

SPLASH!
Muddy water all over Henry.
It was the biggest,
deepest puddle
they had ever seen.
And they loved it.

When Henry's father
called for Henry
and didn't find him,
he went outside.
He looked down the road.
SPLASH! he heard.
He put on his raincoat
and went walking.

SPLASH! he saw.
Henry's father saw Mudge,
with a muddy face
and muddy tail
and muddy in between.

Henry's father saw Henry,
with a muddy face
and muddy shoes
and muddy in between.
And he yelled, *'Henry!'*
No more splashes.
Just a boy and a dog,
dripping.
'Hi Dad,' Henry said,
with a little smile.
Mudge wagged his tail.
'Henry, you know
you should have asked me first,'
Henry's father said.
'I know,' said Henry.

'I am surprised at you,'
Henry's father said.
'I'm sorry,' said Henry.
'I don't know what to do
with you,' Henry's father said.
Henry looked sad.
Then Mudge wagged his tail,
licked Henry's hand,
and shook the water
from his big wet furry body
all over Henry and Henry's father.

'*Mudge*!' Henry yelled.
Henry's father stood there
with a muddy face
and muddy shoes
and muddy in between.
He looked at Mudge,
he looked at Henry,
he looked at the big puddle.

Then he smiled.
'Wow,' he said.
And he jumped in.

He splashed water on Mudge.
He splashed water on Henry.
He said, 'Next time, ask me along!'
Henry said, 'Sure, Dad.'
And Henry splashed him back.

The Kittens

In May the cat who lived
next door to Henry and Mudge
had a litter of kittens.
There were five kittens.
One was orange.
One was grey.
One was black and white.
And two were all black.

The kittens sometimes stayed
in a box on their front step
to get some sun
while the mother cat rested.
One day Henry and Mudge
peeked into the box.
They saw tiny little
kitten faces
and tiny little
kitten paws
and heard tiny little
kitten meows.

Mudge sniffed
and sniffed and sniffed.
He wagged his tail
and sneezed
and sniffed some more.
Then he put his
big head into the box
and with his big tongue
he licked
all five kittens.

Henry laughed.
'Do you want
some kittens of your own?'
he asked Mudge.
Mudge grunted
and wagged his tail again.
Whenever the kittens
were on the front step,
Henry and Mudge
visited the box.
Henry loved their
little noses.
And he had even
given them names.

He called them
Venus,
Earth,
Mars,
Jupiter,
and Saturn.
Henry loved planets, too.

While Henry was at school one day,
a new dog came up Henry's street.
The five kittens
were sleeping
in the box on the step.
Mudge was sleeping in Henry's house.

When the new dog
got closer to Henry's house,
Mudge's ears went up.

When the new dog
got even closer
to Henry's house,
Mudge's nose went in the air.
And just when the new dog
was in front of
Henry's house,
Mudge barked.

He barked and barked
and barked
until Henry's mother
opened the door.

And just as
Mudge ran out the door,
the new dog
was on the neighbour's step,
looking into the kittens' box.
And just as the new dog
was putting his big teeth into the box,
Mudge ran up behind him.

SNAP! went Mudge's teeth
when the new dog saw him.
SNAP! went Mudge's teeth again
when the new dog looked back
at the box of kittens.

Mudge growled.
He looked into the eyes of the new dog.
He stood ready to jump.
And the new dog backed away
from the box.
He didn't want the kittens anymore.
He just wanted to leave.
And he did.

Mudge looked in the kitten box.
He saw five tiny faces
and five skinny tails
and twenty little paws.
He reached in and licked
all five kittens.

Then he lay down
beside the box
and waited for Henry.
Venus,
Earth,
Mars,
Jupiter,
and Saturn
went back to sleep.

Don't miss the next Henry And Mudge adventure
Available now from Pocket Books

Henry and Mudge
Summer Fun

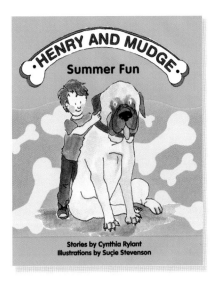

It is summertime and Henry and Mudge share four holiday adventures together in the sun. They make yummy sandwiches for a picnic, have some water fun in the garden, invent a new game and have a great day on the beach. And although all perfect days must end, the two friends will always have each other so there will be lots more adventures to come!

Meet Toby!

The pint-sized star of an exciting new series
Available now from Pocket Books

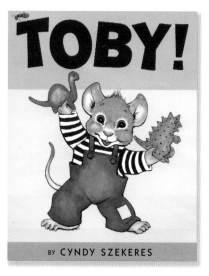

Toby is an energetic, three-and-a-half-year-old mouse in a big world. He is loving, friendly, curious and full of giggles. Parents will recognise their own child in Toby's charming antics and children will laugh at his adventures whilst learning about everyday things with him. Meet this very special mouse in our first story, *Toby!* In *Toby's Alphabet Walk*, he learns his letters with a basketful of outdoor objects. And in *Toby's Rainbow Clothes*, he learns about colours and puts together his very own dazzling outfit. The bright, colourful illustrations coupled with the antics of this very special mouse, make story time (and learning), fun!